STAR WARS
THE BAD BATCH

HUNTED!

Random House 🏠 New York

© & ™ 2022 Lucasfilm Ltd. All rights reserved. Published in the United States by Random House Children's Books, an imprint of Penguin Random House LLC, 1745 Broadway, New York, NY 10019, and in Canada by Penguin Random House Canada Limited, Toronto, in conjunction with Disney Enterprises, Inc. Screen Comix is a trademark of Penguin Random House LLC. Random House and the Random House colophon are registered trademarks of Penguin Random House LLC.

ISBN 978-0-7364-4214-5 (trade) — ISBN 978-0-7364-4229-9 (ebook)

rhcbooks.com

Printed in the United States of America

CLONE FORCE 99 IS A SQUAD OF ELITE AND EXPERIMENTAL CLONE TROOPERS. MEMBERS OF BAD BATCH, AS THEY PREFER TO BE CALLED, EACH POSSESS A SINGULAR EXCEPTIONAL SKILL THAT MAKES THEM EXTRAORDINARILY EFFECTIVE SOLDIERS AND A FORMIDABLE CREW.

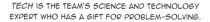

HUNTER, THE LEADER, HAS HEIGHTENED SENSES THAT MAKE HIM AN EXCELLENT TRACKER.

TECH IS THE TEAM'S SCIENCE AND TECHNOLOGY EXPERT WHO HAS A GIFT FOR PROBLEM-SOLVING.

LARGE AND LOUD, *WRECKER* IS SUPER-STRONG AND ESPECIALLY ENJOYS EXPLOSIONS.

A FORMER ARC TROOPER, *ECHO* HAS A SOCKET ARM AND CYBERNETIC IMPLANTS THAT GIVE HIM THE ABILITY TO INTERACT WITH COMPUTER SYSTEMS.

CROSSHAIR, THE SHARPSHOOTER, CAN HIT ANY TARGET. BUT HIS INHIBITOR CHIP MAKES HIM QUESTION WHETHER HIS LOYALTIES ARE WITH HIS TEAM OR THE NEW EMPIRE.

AFTER BEING ARRESTED FOR TREASON, THE BAD BATCH FLEE THE KAMINO BASE WITH A YOUNG CLONE NAMED OMEGA. CROSSHAIR STAYS BEHIND.

IMPERIAL ADMIRAL *TARKIN* ORDERS CROSSHAIR TO HUNT DOWN HIS OLD TEAMMATES.

AND BOUNTY HUNTER *FENNEC SHAND* IS HIRED TO FIND OMEGA AND RETURN HER TO THE CLONERS ON KAMINO.

The Bad Batch and Omega are being **HUNTED***!*

AFTER HAVING THEIR INHIBITOR CHIPS SURGICALLY REMOVED AT A DECOMISSIONED REPUBLIC MEDICAL FACILITY, THE BAD BATCH ARE DISCOVERED BY CROSSHAIR AND A SQUAD OF IMPERIAL STORMTROOPERS.

TAPPING OUR COMMS TO TRACK OUR MOVEMENTS? SO PREDICTABLE.

HA. NICE TO SEE YOU TOO, CROSSHAIR.

ECHO, SCOMP IN AND REROUTE RESERVE POWER TO THE CANNONS.

IF THESE CANNONS FIRE, THIS WHOLE DECK WILL COLLAPSE.

EXACTLY.

LOOK AT YOU ALL, SCAVENGING LIKE RATS. HOW PATHETIC.

5

13

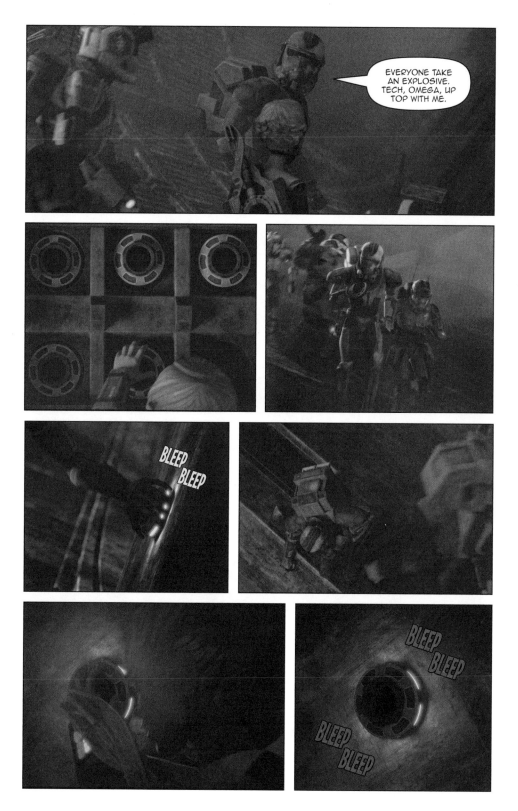

18

19

21

22

23

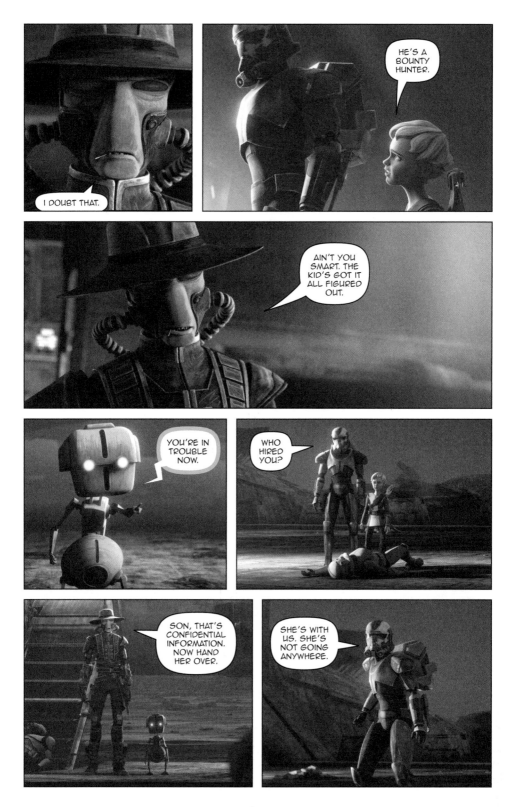

24

25

CAD BANE'S SHIP

LET ME OUT OF HERE!

AFRAID NOT.

LOOKING FOR YOUR COMMUNICATION DEVICE? IT HAS BEEN CONFISCATED AND PLACED IN A SECURE COMPARTMENT.

I SAID LET ME OUT OF HERE.

ON KAMINO

I WILL DELIVER THE PAYMENT AND RETRIEVE OMEGA.

YOUR PERSONAL INTEREST IN THE YOUNG CLONE HAS THREATENED OUR OPERATION ENOUGH.

TAUN WE, YOU WILL GO TO OUR ABANDONED FACILITY ON BORA VIO. BRING THE BOUNTY HUNTER HIS PAYMENT AND RECOVER OUR PROPERTY.

YES, PRIME MINISTER.

WHEN THE CLONE IS RETURNED, CONFINE HER TO THE SUB-LEVEL FACILITY. ONCE YOU HAVE RETRIEVED THE GENETIC MATERIAL NEEDED, TERMINATE HER.

34

MEANWHILE...

THIS IS ALL THAT CLONE'S FAULT. HE SHOT MY LEG OFF!

HE WAS PROTECTING ME. THAT'S WHAT FRIENDS DO. WHY ISN'T YOURS HELPING YOU?

WELL, MR. BANE IS VERY BUSY.

OMEGA SPIES A USEFUL TOOL...

I COULD FIX YOUR LEG IF YOU WANT. IT'S A SIMPLE BOOSTER ADJUSTMENT. I'VE DONE IT A BUNCH OF TIMES FOR AZI-3 BACK ON KAMINO.

AHA. I AM A TECHNO SERVICE DROID. I AM QUITE CAPABLE OF COMPLETING MY OWN REPAIRS. *YOU* ARE A PRISONER AND ARE NOT TO BE TRUSTED.

HAVE IT YOUR WAY.

FIRST THE BOUNTY HUNTER ON PANTORA, AND NOW THIS GUY? WHY ARE THEY AFTER THE KID?

BECAUSE SHE IS MORE VALUABLE THAN WE REALIZED.

WHAT DO YOU MEAN?

I FURTHER ANALYZED OMEGA'S GENETIC PROFILE AND DISCOVERED SHE HAS PURE FIRST-GENERATION DNA.

WHOA...WAIT...WHAT DOES THAT MEAN?

ALL CLONES WERE CREATED FROM A HOST NAMED JANGO FETT. WHILE OUR GENETIC STRUCTURE WAS MODIFIED FOR GROWTH ACCELERATION AND OBEDIENCE, OMEGA IS A PURE GENETIC REPLICATION.

HOW MANY CLONES LIKE THAT EXIST?

TO MY KNOWLEDGE, THERE'S ONLY ONE OTHER: A MALE CLONE, CODE NAME ALPHA, LATER REFERRED TO AS BOBA.

SINCE HE DISAPPEARED AT THE START OF THE WAR, THAT MAKES OMEGA THE SOLE LIVING SOURCE OF FETT'S RAW GENETIC MATERIAL.

IF SHE'S VITAL TO THE KAMINOANS' CLONING OPERATION, THEY MUST HAVE PUT THE BOUNTY ON HER.

SO HOW DO WE FIND THIS BOUNTY HUNTER?

TECH, CHECK WITH CID. SEE IF HER CONTACTS KNOW ANYTHING. WE'LL KEEP MONITORING COMMS.

42

43

44

HELLO?
IS ANYONE
THERE? CAN YOU
HEAR ME?

ON THE *MARAUDER*

CID KNOWS ALL
ABOUT BANE, BUT NOT
HOW TO FIND HIM. SHE
SAID WE'RE ON
OUR OWN.

COME IN. COME IN.
ANYONE?

OMEGA?!

47

48

50

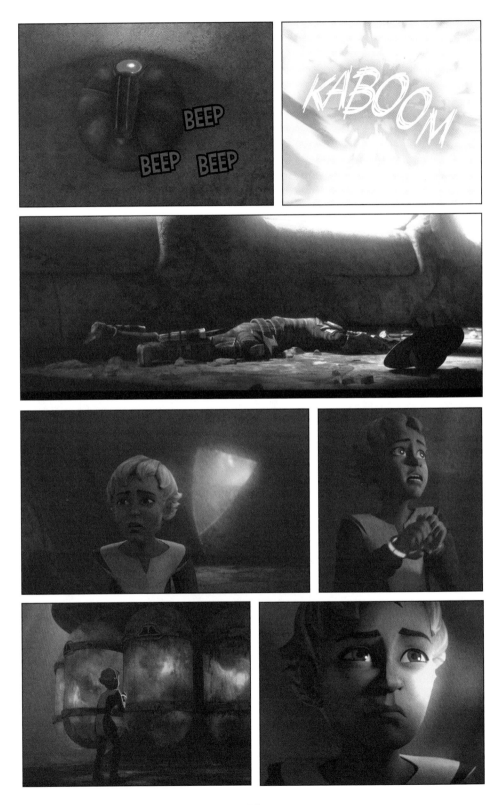

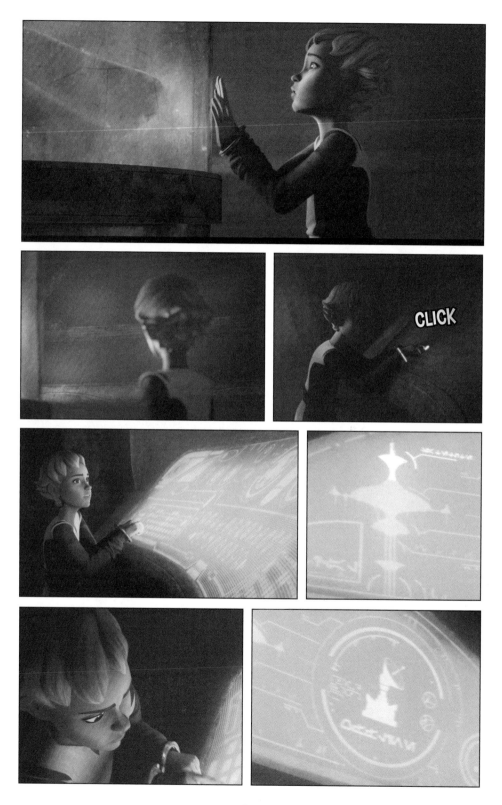

I THINK I'VE GOT HER. SHE'S IN THE LIDO SYSTEM.

WHERE IN THE LIDO SYSTEM?

I'M PINPOINTING THE EXACT COORDINATES. HANG ON!

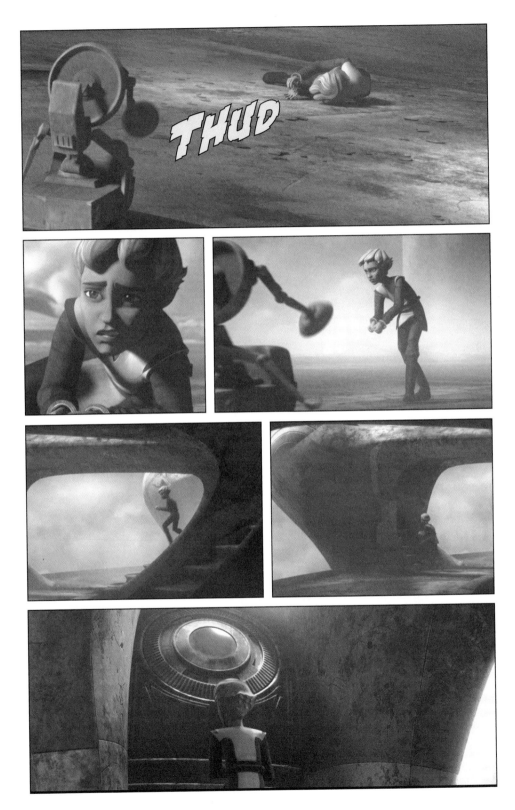

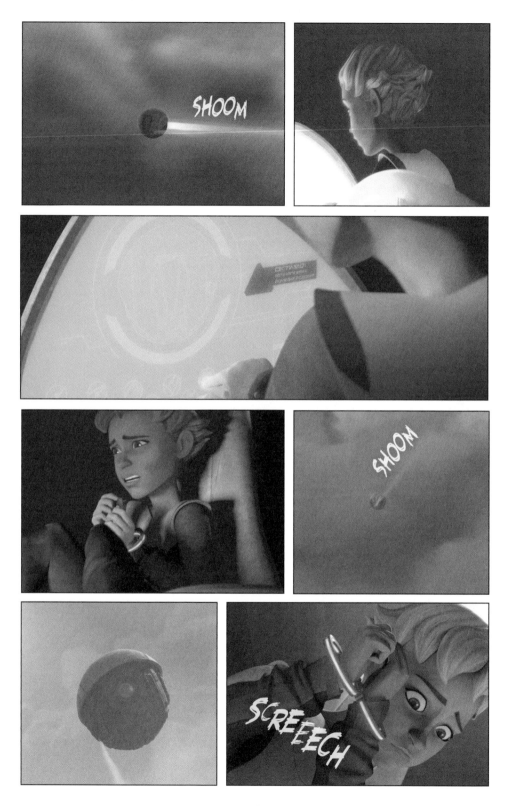

ON THE *MARAUDER*

CAN'T
SLEEP?

I KEEP THINKING ABOUT
THE KAMINOANS. SEEING THAT
PLACE...I DON'T WANT TO END UP
AN EXPERIMENT IN A TUBE.

THAT'S
NOT GOING TO
HAPPEN.

IF I'M AS VALUABLE AS YOU
SAY, LAMA SU WILL KEEP SENDING
BOUNTY HUNTERS AFTER ME.

Created by Dave Filoni
Based on STAR WARS and characters created by George Lucas

Developed by
Dave Filoni
Jennifer Corbett

Supervising Director: Brad Rau

Executive Producer: Dave Filoni

Executive Producer: Athena Yvette Portillo

Executive Producers
Jennifer Corbett
Brad Rau

Co-Executive Producer: Carrie Beck
Producer: Josh Rimes
Associate Producer: Alex Spotswood

Episode 8: Reunion
Directed by Steward Lee
Written by Christian Taylor
Story Editor: Matt Michnovetz

Episode 9: Bounty Lost
Directed by Brad Rau and Nathaniel Villanueva
Written by Matt Michnovetz
Story Editor: Matt Michnovetz

For Lucasfilm
Senior Editor: Robert Simpson
Creative Director: Michael Siglain
Art Director: Troy Alders
Project Manager, Digital and Video Assets: LeAndre Thomas
Lucasfilm Art Department: Phil Szostak
Lucasfilm Story Group: Pablo Hidalgo, Matt Martin, and Emily Shkoukani